This igloo book belongs to:

....

igloobooks

Published in 2017
by Igloo Books Ltd
Cottage Farm
Sywell
NN6 0BJ
www.igloobooks.com

STA002 0717
4 6 8 10 9 7 5
ISBN 978-1-78197-466-7

Illustrated by Louise Forshaw

Printed and manufactured in China

PUPPY LOVE

igloobooks

I got my dog, Little Paws, for my last birthday.
He jumped out of the box because he couldn't wait to play.

Mum and Dad shouted, "Surprise! This is your new pup."
He looked so cute sitting there, in a big bow, all wrapped up.

I thought that Little Paws was the perfect present for me,
But I didn't know how much trouble, one tiny dog could be.

Every day he wakes me up, early in the morning,
Licking my face all over, when I'm still busy yawning.

When Little Paws sees the sun outside, he wants to go and explore.
He sits on the mat, wags his tail and waits patiently by the door.

"Woof," he barks, looking at me. "It's time, come on, let's go!"
When I see those big puppy-dog eyes, I just can't say no.

Little Paws tries to be good, when we reach the park,
But when he sees the fluffy ducks, he just has to bark.

He chases them across the grass, until they fly up high,
Woofing at them as they escape, into the big, blue sky.

When we pass puddles of mud on the winding path,
Little Paws loves to jump into them for a nice dirt bath.

He jumps and rolls and runs about, while I just stand and frown,
Until his fur turns from golden to a yucky, dark brown.

We have to sneak into the house when Little Paws is mucky,
Hoping Mom and Dad won't see us, if we're really lucky!

We tiptoe quiet as two mice, through hallways and open doors,
Trailing mud all through the house with those little, muddy paws.

I give Little Paws a wash to scrub all the dirt away,
But then he shakes his wet fur coat and water starts to spray.

I cover myself with my hands and yell, "Little Paws, NO!"
But I can't help laughing when I'm soaked from head to toe.

When I go off to school each day, Little Paws misses me,
But he tries not to be naughty and just waits patiently.

Then he gets bored and wants to play with whatever he finds,
Chewing on everything he sees and hoping that no-one minds.

When Mom and Dad see the mess, they get really mad.
They send Little Paws to the corner, where he looks so sad.

He sits still and tries to catch the eyes of people walking past,
Wagging his tail cheekily, until someone smiles at last.

Little Paws is cute, even when he's done something wrong.
Just one look at that cheeky face and we can't stay mad for long.

We all love my dog, Little Paws, just like he's one of us.
Except for one furry ginger cat, and that is grumpy Gus.

Cuddled up together, when the day comes to an end,
I know Little Paws loves me, too. He's my furry best friend.